Dear Parent:

Your child's love of reading starts here!

Every child learns to read in a different way and at his or her own speed. Some go back and forth between reading levels and read favorite books again and again. Others read through each level in order. You can help your young reader improve and become more confident by encouraging his or her own interests and abilities. From books your child reads with you to the first books he or she reads alone, there are I Can Read Books for every stage of reading:

SHARED READING
Basic language, word repetition, and whimsical illustrations, ideal for sharing with your emergent reader

BEGINNING READING
Short sentences, familiar words, and simple concepts for children eager to read on their own

READING WITH HELP
Engaging stories, longer sentences, and language play for developing readers

READING ALONE
Complex plots, challenging vocabulary, and high-interest topics for the independent reader

I Can Read Books have introduced children to the joy of reading since 1957. Featuring award-winning authors and illustrators and a fabulous cast of beloved characters, I Can Read Books set the standard for beginning readers.

A lifetime of discovery begins with the magical words "I Can Read!"

Visit www.icanread.com for information
on enriching your child's reading experience.

MONSTER TRUCK

BY MERCER MAYER

HARPER
An Imprint of HarperCollinsPublishers

To Evangeline,
my new granddaughter,
who always steals my crackers.

I Can Read® and I Can Read Book® are trademarks of HarperCollins Publishers.

Little Critter: Monster Truck

www.icanread.com

ISBN 978-0-06-243149-3 (trade bdg.) — ISBN 978-0-06-243148-6 (pbk.)

23 24 25 26 27 LB 10 9 8 7 6 5 4 3 2 1 ❖ First Edition

   A Big Tuna Trading Company, LLC/J. R. Sansevere Book
www.littlecritter.com

Tiger came over to play with
his new monster truck.

It was called The Squisher.

It was so cool!

I ran inside and asked my dad,
"Can I get the new Squisher too?"

"What's wrong with
your old truck?" asked Dad.
"I got it when I was a baby!"
I said.

"Okay," said Dad.
"But you have to do
extra chores for two weeks
to help pay for it."

I worked hard.

I let the dog out.

I took out the trash.

I cleaned my room really well.

I set the table.

I took a bath without a fuss.

Finally I had the money.

Dad drove me to the toy store.

But when we got there,
the Squisher was sold out.
"No fair!" I said.

15

"Wait," said Dad.
"Your uncle Zeb is in
the Monster Truck Rally.

He drives a real monster truck.

Let's go!"

17

We had second-row seats.

But I couldn't see very well.

I got popcorn.

Dad got a corn dog.

19

Uncle Zeb did the best tricks.

He drove on two wheels.

Everybody screamed.
I got so excited,
I spilled my popcorn!

Before I knew it,
the rally was over.
"Let's go see Uncle Zeb!"
said Dad.

And then I got to ride.
We zoomed!

But that wasn't all!
Uncle Zeb said,
"I have a surprise for you."
He gave me a big box!

I opened the box.
It was a red monster truck,
just like Uncle Zeb's.

"I got you the last one from the toy store," said Uncle Zeb.

When we got home,
I ran inside.

I called Tiger.

"Can you come over to play?"
I asked.

Tiger and I played
with our monster trucks.

That night, I dreamed about
being a monster truck driver
when I grew up.